Before reading

Look at the book cover to
Ask, "What do you think w

To build independence, th
at the start of this book. If
back to pages 6 and 7 in
the child.

During reading

Offer plenty of support and praise as the child reads the story.
Listen carefully and respond to events in the text.

In 8c, the new **Key Words** are not shown at the bottom of
the page. If the child hesitates over a word, turn to the back
of the book to practise reading it together. If the word is
phonically decodable, you can sound out the letters and
blend the sounds to read the word ("d-o-g, dog"). Praise the
child for their effort, then return to the story.

Pause every few pages and ask questions to check the child's
understanding of what they have read. If they begin to lose
concentration, stop reading and save the page for later.

Celebrate the child's achievement and come back to the
story the next day.

After reading

After reading this book, ask, "Did you enjoy the story? What did
you like about it?" Encourage the child to share their opinions.

Use the comprehension questions on page 54 to check the
child's understanding and recall of the text.

Ladybird

Series Consultant: Professor David Waugh
With thanks to Kulwinder Maude

LADYBIRD BOOKS

UK | USA | Canada | Ireland | Australia
India | New Zealand | South Africa

Ladybird Books is part of the Penguin Random House group of companies
whose addresses can be found at global.penguinrandomhouse.com.
www.penguin.co.uk   www.puffin.co.uk   www.ladybird.co.uk

Original edition of Key Words with Peter and Jane first published by Ladybird Books Ltd 1964
Series updated 2023
This book first published 2023
001

Text copyright © Ladybird Books Ltd, 1964, 2023
Illustrations by Flora Aranyi
Based on characters and design by Gustavo Mazali
Illustrations copyright © Ladybird Books Ltd, 2023

With thanks to Liz Pemberton for her contributions in advising on the illustrations
With thanks to Inclusive Minds for connecting us with their Inclusion Ambassador network,
and in particular thanks to Guntaas Kaur Chugh for her input on the illustrations

Printed in China

The authorized representative in the EEA is Penguin Random House Ireland,
Morrison Chambers, 32 Nassau Street, Dublin D02 YH68

A CIP catalogue record for this book is available from the British Library

ISBN: 978–0–241–51096–4

All correspondence to:
Ladybird Books
Penguin Random House Children's
One Embassy Gardens, 8 Viaduct Gardens, London SW11 7BW

MIX
Paper from
responsible sources
FSC® C018179

Key Words

with Peter and Jane

8c

The pool party

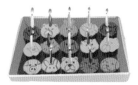

Based on the original
Key Words with Peter and Jane
reading scheme and research by William Murray

Original edition written by William Murray
This edition written by Shari Last
Illustrated by Flora Aranyi
Based on characters and design by Gustavo Mazali

Jane was at the swimming pool.
She liked going to the pool every
week because she liked swimming.
She was very good at it.

Peter liked going to the pool
every week because he had fun
splashing about with his mum.

"Peter," said Mum, "we are going to surprise Jane for her birthday."

"I like surprises!" said Peter.

"Jane likes coming to the pool," Mum said. "Let's give her a surprise pool party!"

"Yes!" said Peter. "Jane will really like that for her birthday."

At home, Peter helped Dad to plan Jane's surprise party when she was playing in the garden.

"The party is one week away. Jane's friends will meet us at the swimming pool," Dad said. "We will play many party games."

"Jane will be so surprised," said Peter.

Peter and Jane played football in the garden.

"It's my birthday next week," said Jane. "What can we do for my birthday party?"

"Your birthday party?" asked Peter.

"Yes!" said Jane. "I will find Mum and ask if we can go to Granny and Grandad's house."

"Good plan," said Peter. He liked knowing about Jane's surprise pool party.

It was the day before Jane's surprise pool party. Jane was playing with Will next door.

Dad had asked Peter to find Jane's swim bag, because he wanted to put her swimming clothes in it.

Peter gave the bag to Dad.

"Good boy, Peter!" said Dad.

"You are good at surprises," said Mum.

15

"As Jane is next door, let's make things for the party," said Dad. "I will make buns."

Dad's buns had baby animals on them.

"We must put them away where Jane can't find them," said Peter.

Mum had many games to play at the party.

"I will put the party things in the car before it's time to go," she said.

When Jane was home, she set out her best clothes for the next day.

"Before I go to bed, I am putting out my birthday clothes," said Jane.

"You might get some clothes for your birthday," said Peter.

The next day, Jane jumped out of her bed and on to Peter's bed!

"I am the birthday girl today!" she yelled. "I am a year older."

"Here is your birthday card!" said Peter.

"Thank you, Peter. What are we doing today?" asked Jane.

"I don't know," said Peter.

"It's your birthday today, Jane!" said Mum and Dad. They gave the birthday girl a big hug.

Mum, Dad and Peter gave Jane three birthday gifts.

"You gave me a bear, Peter! Thank you," said Jane.

"Do you want to go to Granny and Grandad's house today?" asked Dad.

"Yes, please!" said Jane.

23

In the car, Jane was surprised when Mum turned left at the top of the street.

"Granny and Grandad don't live here, Mum," said Jane. "This is the swimming pool. Are we going here before Granny's?"

"Surprise!" yelled Peter, Mum and Dad.

Jane saw her friends waiting for her next to the pool. "Surprise!" they all said.

Pippa gave Jane a card with three horses on it.

"They are your three horses, Pippa!" Jane said. "Thank you for drawing them for me."

Will gave Jane a big round float for her birthday. "We can play on it in the pool!" he said to Jane.

"You all gave me so many birthday gifts. Thank you!" said Jane.

Next, the children put on their swimming clothes.

"Let's go in the pool now!" said Jane.

The children splashed in the pool. Jane had her round float from Will.

"Are you having a good party so far?" asked Naz.

"Yes!" said Jane. "You all gave me a very big surprise."

"When you are all in the pool, it will be time for the first game. First, every boy and girl must find a toy," said Dad.

The children saw many pool toys next to the baby pool. They all picked up toys and jumped into the pool again.

Peter had a football, and Jane had a toy boat.

31

"Next, you must swim to the end and put the toys in that big round tub there," said Dad. "And . . . go!"

Peter was slower than the older children. Mum walked next to him and cheered for him.

Jane was very quick. She was the first to get her toy in the round tub.

33

Next, they played in the pool with the football.

When it was their turn, the children had to hit the football away.
The football splashed in the water many times.

"Hit it away!" yelled Peter.

Pippa jumped up and hit the football away.

"Good work, Pippa!" Peter said.

After the game with the football, there was time for one more swim in the pool.

"Amber and I are going to play in the baby pool with Maya," said Peter.

"Can I play with my round float that Will gave me?" Jane said.

"Here it is," said Dad. "You can play round here with it."

Next, it was time to have something to eat in the garden. The children put on their party clothes.

They sat in the garden next to the swimming pool, and Mum and Dad gave them many things to eat and drink.

"When you are full, you can draw pictures and play with the football," Mum said to Jane's friends.

39

Mum walked out of the pool door with the birthday buns.

"The buns have sweet baby animals on them," said Pippa. "I can see three kinds of animals – a baby dog, a baby cat and a baby rabbit."

"I like baby animals!" Jane said.

When Jane's friends left, Jane, Peter, Mum and Dad put the party things away.

"Thank you," said Jane. "I had the best time at my pool party today. It was a very good surprise. First, we had fun in the pool, and next, we had fun in the garden."

"It has been fun to surprise you!" said Peter.

At home, Peter and Jane played in their garden.

"Let's draw some pictures of today," said Jane.

"I am going to draw the football game in the pool," said Peter. "I'll draw the football splashing down on the water."

"I will draw the pool with all my friends in it," said Jane. "I'll be on the round float that Will gave me."

Amber, Will and Maya popped up from their garden next door.

"That was a very good birthday party today!" said Will. "The best part of the day was playing with the football in the pool."

"I liked the baby pool," said Amber.

"And me!" said Maya.

"I liked it when you all gave me a big surprise!" said Jane.

"Thank you for a very good day today," said Jane, before getting into bed.

Mum and Dad gave the birthday girl one more hug.

"I had been wanting a pool party," said Jane.

"Yes, we have been going to the pool for many years now," said Mum. "You liked it as a baby, Jane."

49

"Here is a picture of your first time at the pool," said Dad. "You jumped in!"

Jane was very little in Dad's picture. She was splashing in the baby pool.

"You had to be the first baby to get in the pool every time," said Mum.

"It's a baby pool party!" said Peter.

It had been a fun day, full of surprises.

Before bed, Peter said, "That was a really good birthday, Jane. You are very old now!"

"This was my best birthday yet," said Jane. "Now I have to wait one more year before the next one!"

Questions

Answer these questions about
the story.

1 Why are Peter, Mum and Dad
planning a surprise pool party
for Jane?

2 What does Peter do when Jane is
playing with Will next door?

3 What does Peter give Jane for
her birthday?

4 What do the children do after
swimming?

5 What does Dad show Jane and
Peter at the end of the story?